Henry Brooke, Edward Moore

Fables for the Female Sex

Fourth Edition

Henry Brooke, Edward Moore

Fables for the Female Sex
Fourth Edition

ISBN/EAN: 9783744768092

Printed in Europe, USA, Canada, Australia, Japan

Cover: Foto ©Andreas Hilbeck / pixelio.de

More available books at **www.hansebooks.com**

F. Hayman inv.t et delin. S. F. Ravenet Sculp.

ABLES

FOR THE

FEMALE SEX.

THE FOURTH EDITION.

LONDON:

Printed for T. Davies, in Ruſſell-Street, Covent-Garden; and J. Dodsley, in Pall-Mall.

MDCCLXXI.

PREFACE.

THE *following* FABLES *were written at intervals, when I found myself in humour, and disengaged from matters of great moment. As they are the writings of an idle hour, so they are intended for the reading of those, whose only business is amusement. My hopes of profit, or applause, are not immoderate; nor have I printed thro' necessity, or request of friends. I have leave from her* Royal Highness *to address her, and I claim the Fair for my Readers. My fears are lighter than my expectations; I wrote to please myself, and I publish to please others; and this so universally, that I have not wish'd for correctness to rob the critic of his censure, or my friend of the laugh.*

MY intimates are few, and I am not solicious to increase them. I have learnt, that where the writer would please, the man should be unknown. An author is the reverse of all other objects, and magnifies by distance, but diminishes by approach. His private attachments must give place to public favour; for no man can forgive his friend the ill-natured attempt of being thought wiser than himself.

TO avoid therefore the misfortunes that may attend me from any accidental success, I think it necessary to inform those who know me, that I have been assisted in the following papers by the author of Gustavus Vasa. *Let the crime of pleasing be his, whose talents as a writer, and whose virtues as a man, have rendered him a living affront to the whole circle of his acquaintance.*

TABLE OF CONTENTS.

FABLE I.

FABLE II.

FABLE III.

FABLE

FABLE IV.

FABLE V.

FABLE VI.

FABLE VII.

FABLE VIII.

FABLE IX.

FABLE X.

TABLE *of* CONTENTS.

Hayman inv. et del.   C. Mosley sculp.

FABLE I.

The EAGLE, *and the Assembly of* BIRDS.

To her Royal Highness the Princess of *WALES.*

THE moral lay, to beauty due,
I write, *Fair Excellence*, to you;
Well pleas'd to hope my vacant hours
Have been employ'd to sweeten yours.
Truth under fiction I impart,
To weed out folly from the heart,
And shew the paths, that lead astray
The wand'ring nymph from wisdom's way.

I flatter none. The great and good
Are by their actions underſtood;
Your monument if actions raiſe,
Shall I deface by idle praiſe?
I echo not the voice of Fame,
That dwells delighted on your name;
Her friendly tale, however true,
Were flatt'ry, if I told it you.

The proud, the envious, and the vain,
The jilt, the prude, demand my ſtrain;
To theſe, deteſting praiſe, I write,
And vent, in charity, my ſpite,
With friendly hand I hold the glaſs
To all, promiſcuous as they paſs;
Should folly there her likeneſs view,
I fret not that the mirror's true;

If

If the fantaſtic form offend,
I made it not, but would amend.
  Virtue, in every clime and age,
Spurns at the folly-ſoothing page,
While ſatire, that offends the ear
Of vice and paſſion, pleaſes her.
  Premiſing this, your anger ſpare,
And claim the fable, you, who dare.

THE birds in place, by factions preſs'd,
To Jupiter their pray'rs addreſs'd;
By ſpecious lies the ſtate was vex'd,
Their counſels libellers perplex'd;
They begg'd (to ſtop ſeditious tongues)
A gracious hearing of their wrongs.

Jove grants their ſuit. The Eagle ſate,
Decider of the grand debate.

The Pye, to truſt and pow'r preferr'd,
Demands permiſſion to be heard.
Says he, prolixity of phraſe
You know I hate. This libel ſays,
" Some birds there are, who prone to noiſe,
" Are hir'd to ſilence wiſdom's voice,
" And ſkill'd to chatter out the hour,
" Riſe by their emptineſs to pow'r."
That this is aim'd direct at me,
No doubt, you'll readily agree;
Yet well this ſage aſſembly knows,
By parts to government I roſe;
My prudent counſels prop the ſtate;
Magpies were never known to prate.

The Kite rose up. His honest heart
In virtue's suff'rings bore a part.
That there were birds of prey he knew;
So far the libeller said true;
" Voracious, bold, to rapine prone,
" Who knew no int'rest but their own;
" Who hov'ring o'er the farmer's yard,
" Nor pigeon, chick, nor duckling spar'd.
This might be true, but if apply'd
To him, in troth, the sland'rer ly'd.
Since ign'rance then might be misled,
Such things, he thought, were best unsaid.

The Crow was vex'd. As yester-morn
He flew across the new-sown corn,
A screaming boy was set for pay,
He knew, to drive the crows away;

Scandal had found him out in turn,
And buzz'd abroad, that crows love corn.

The Owl arose, with solemn face,
And thus harangu'd upon the case.
That magpies prate, it may be true,
A kite may be voracious too,
Crows sometimes deal in new-sown pease;
He libels not, who strikes at these;
The slander's here—" But there are birds,
" Whose wisdom lies in looks, not words;
" Blund'rers, who level in the dark,
" And always shoot beside the mark."
He names not me; but these are hints,
Which manifest at whom he squints;
I were indeed that blund'ring fowl,
To question if he meant an owl.

Ye wretches, hence! the Eagle cries,
'Tis conſcience, conſcience that applies;
The virtuous mind takes no alarm,
Secur'd by innocence from harm;
While guilt, and his aſſociate fear,
Are ſtartled at the paſſing air.

Tab. 2.

F Hayman inv — C Grignion sculp

FABLE II.

The PANTHER, *the* HORSE, *and other* BEASTS.

THE man, who ſeeks to win the fair,
(So cuſtom ſays) muſt truth forbear;
Muſt fawn and flatter, cringe and lie,
And raiſe the goddeſs to the ſky.
For truth is hateful to her ear,
A rudeneſs, which ſhe cannot bear.
A rudeneſs? Yes. I ſpeak my thoughts;
For truth upbraids her with her faults.

How wretched, Cloe, then am I,
Who love you, and yet cannot lie!
And ſtill to make you leſs my friend,
I ſtrive your errors to amend!

But

But ſhall the ſenſeleſs fop impart
The ſofteſt paſſion to your heart,
While he, who tells you honeſt truth,
And points to happineſs your youth,
Determines, by his care, his lot,
And lives neglected and forgot?

Truſt me, my dear, with greater eaſe
Your taſte for flatt'ry I could pleaſe,
And ſimilies in each dull line,
Like glow-worms in the dark, ſhould ſhine.
What if I ſay your lips diſcloſe
The freſhneſs of the op'ning roſe?
Or that your cheeks are beds of flow'rs,
Enripen'd by refreſhing ſhow'rs?
Yet certain as theſe flow'rs ſhall fade,
Time every beauty will invade.

The

The butterfly, of various hue,
More than the flow'r resembles you;
Fair, flutt'ring, fickle, busy thing.
To pleasure ever on the wing,
Gayly coquetting for an hour,
To die, and ne'er be thought of more.

Would you the bloom of youth should last?
'Tis virtue that must bind it fast;
An easy carriage, wholly free
From sour reserve, or levity;
Good-natur'd mirth, an open heart,
And looks unskill'd in any art;
Humility, enough to own
The frailties, which a friend makes known,
And decent pride, enough to know
The worth, that virtue can bestow.

These

These are the charms, which ne'er decay,
Though youth, and beauty fade away,
And time, which all things elſe removes,
Still heightens virtue, and improves.

You'll frown, and aſk, To what intent
This blunt addreſs to you is ſent?
I'll ſpare the queſtion, and confeſs
I'd praiſe you, if I lov'd you leſs;
But rail, be angry, or complain,
I will be rude, while you are vain.

BENEATH a lion's peaceful reign,
When beaſts met friendly on the plain,
A Panther of majeſtic port,
(The vaineſt female of the court)

With

With ſpotted ſkin, and eyes of fire,
Fill'd every boſom with deſire.
Where e'er ſhe mov'd, a ſervile crowd
Of fawning creatures cring'd and bow'd:
Aſſemblies every week ſhe held,
(Like modern belles) with coxcombs fill'd,
Where noiſe, and nonſenſe, and grimace,
And lies and ſcandal fill'd the place.

Behold the gay, fantaſtic thing,
Encircled by the ſpacious ring.
Low-bowing, with important look,
As firſt in rank, the Monkey ſpoke.
" Gad take me, madam, but I ſwear,
" No angel ever look'd ſo fair:
" Forgive my rudeneſs, but I vow,
" You were not quite divine till now;

" Thoſe

" Those limbs! that shape! and then those eyes!
" O, close them, or the gazer dies!"

Nay, gentle pug, for goodness hush,
I vow, and swear, you make me blush;
I shall be angry at this rate;
'Tis so like flatt'ry, which I hate.

The Fox, in deeper cunning vers'd,
The beauties of her mind rehears'd,
And talk'd of knowledge, taste, and sense,
To which the fair have vast pretence!
Yet well he knew them always vain
Of what they strive not to attain,
And play'd so cunningly his part,
That pug was rival'd in his art.

The Goat avow'd his am'rous flame,
And burnt—for what he durst not name;

Yet hop'd a meeting in the wood
Might make his meaning underſtood.
Half angry at the bold addreſs,
She frown'd; but yet ſhe muſt confeſs,
Such beauties might inflame his blood,
But ſtill his phraſe was ſomewhat rude.
  The Hog her neatneſs much admir'd;
The formal Aſs her ſwiftneſs fir'd;
While all to feed her folly ſtrove,
And by their praiſes ſhar'd her love.
  The Horſe, whoſe generous heart diſdain'd
Applauſe, by ſervile flatt'ry gain'd,
With graceful courage, ſilence broke,
And thus with indignation ſpoke.
  When flatt'ring monkeys fawn and prate,
They juſtly raiſe contempt, or hate;

For

For merit's turn'd to ridicule,
Applauded by the grinning fool.
The artful fox your wit commends,
To lure you to his ſelfiſh ends;
From the vile flatt'rer turn away,
For knaves make friendſhips to betray.
Diſmiſs the train of fops, and fools,
And learn to live by wiſdom's rules;
Such beauties might the lion warm,
Did not your folly break the charm;
For who would court that lovely ſhape,
To be the rival of an ape?
He ſaid, and ſnorting in diſdain,
Spurn'd at the crowd, and ſought the plain.

F Hayman inv C Grignion Sculp

FABLE III.

The NIGHTINGALE *and* GLOW-WORM.

THE prudent nymph, whose cheeks disclose
The lilly, and the blushing rose,
From public view her charms will screen,
And rarely in the crowd be seen;
This simple truth shall keep her wise,
"The fairest fruits attract the flies."

ONE night a Glow-worm, proud and vain,
Contemplating her glitt'ring train,

Cry'd, ſure there never was in nature
So elegant, ſo fine a creature.
All other inſects, that I ſee,
The frugal ant, induſtrious bee,
Or ſilk-worm, with contempt I view;
With all that low, mechanic crew,
Who ſervilely their lives employ
In buſineſs, enemy to joy.
Mean, vulgar herd! ye are my ſcorn,
For grandeur only I was born,
Or ſure am ſprung from race divine,
And plac'd on earth, to live and ſhine.
Thoſe lights, that ſparkle ſo on high,
Are but the glow-worms of the ſky,
And kings on earth their gems admire,
Becauſe they imitate my fire.

She

She ſpoke. Attentive on a ſpray,
A Nightingale forbore his lay;
He ſaw the ſhining morſel near,
And flew, directed by the glare;
A while he gaz'd with ſober look,
And thus the trembling prey beſpoke.

Deluded fool, with pride elate,
Know, 'tis thy beauty brings thy fate:
Leſs dazzling, long thou might'ſt have lain
Unheeded on the velvet plain:
Pride, ſoon or late, degraded mourns,
And beauty wrecks whom ſhe adorns.

1.

20

Tab. 4.

F Hayman inv C Grignion Sculp

FABLE IV.

HYMEN, *and* DEATH.

SIXTEEN, dy'e ſay? Nay then 'tis time,
Another year deſtroys your prime.
But ſtay—the ſettlement! " That's made."
Why then's my ſimple girl afraid?
Yet hold a moment, if you can,
And heedfully the fable ſcan.

THE ſhades were fled, the morning bluſh'd,
The winds were in their caverns huſh'd

When Hymen, pensive and sedate,
Held o'er the fields his musing gait.
Behind him, through the green-wood shade,
Death's meagre form the god survey'd;
Who quickly, with gigantic stride,
Out-went his pace and join'd his side.
The chat on various subjects ran,
Till angry Hymen thus began.

Relentless Death, whose iron sway
Mortal reluctant must obey,
Still of thy pow'r shall I complain,
And thy too partial hand arraign?
When Cupid brings a pair of hearts,
All over stuck with equal darts,
Thy cruel shafts my hopes deride,
And cut the knot that Hymen ty'd.

Shall not the bloody, and the bold,
The miser, hoarding up his gold,
The harlot, reeking from the stew,
Alone thy fell revenge pursue?
But must the gentle, and the kind,
Thy fury, undistinguish'd, find?

The monarch calmly thus reply'd;
Weigh well the cause, and then decide.
That friend of yours you lately nam'd,
Cupid, alone is to be blam'd;
Then let the charge be justly laid;
That idle boy neglects his trade,
And hardly once in twenty years,
A couple to your temple bears.
The wretches, whom your office blends,
Silenus now, or Plutus sends;

Hence care, and bitterneſs, and ſtrife,
Are common to the nuptial life.

Believe me; more than all mankind,
Your vot'ries my compaſſion find;
Yet cruel am I call'd, and baſe,
Who ſeek the wretched to releaſe;
The captive from his bonds to free,
Indiſſoluble but for me.

'Tis I entice him to the yoke;
By me, your crowded altars ſmoke:
For mortals boldly dare the nooſe,
Secure that Death will ſet them looſe.

24

Tab. 2.

F. Hayman inv. C. Grignion sc

FABLE V.

The POET, *and his* PATRON.

WHY, Cœlia, is your ſpreading waiſt
So looſe, ſo negligently lac'd?
Why muſt the wrapping bed-gown hide
Your ſnowy boſom's ſwelling pride?
How ill that dreſs adorns your head,
Diſtain'd, and rumpled from the bed!
Thoſe clouds, that ſhade your blooming face,
A little water might diſplace,

As Nature every morn bestows
The crystal dew, to cleanse the rose.
Those tresses, as the raven black,
That wav'd in ringlets down your back,
Uncomb'd, and injured by neglect,
Destroy the face, which once they deck'd.
  Whence this forgetfulness of dress?
Pray, madam, are you married?—Yes,
Nay, then indeed the wonder ceases,
No matter now how loose your dress is;
The end is won, your fortune's made,
Your sister now may take the trade.
  Alas! what pity 'tis to find
This fault in half the female kind!
From hence proceed aversion, strife,
And all that sours the wedded life.

Beauty

Beauty can only point the dart,
'Tis neatneſs guides it to the heart;
Let neatneſs then, and beauty ſtrive
To keep a wav'ring flame alive.
'Tis harder far (you'll find it true)
To keep the conqueſt, than ſubdue;
Admit us once behind the ſcreen
What is there farther to be ſeen?
A newer face may raiſe the flame,
But every woman is the ſame.
Then ſtudy chiefly to improve
The charm, that fix'd your huſband's love.
Weigh well his humour. Was it dreſs,
That gave your beauty power to bleſs?
Purſue it ſtill; be neater ſeen;
'Tis always frugal to be clean;

So ſhall you keep alive deſire,
And time's ſwift wing ſhall fan the fire.

IN garret high (as ſtories ſay)
A Poet ſung his tuneful lay;
So ſoft, ſo ſmooth his verſe, you'd ſwear
Apollo, and the Muſes there;
Thro' all the town his praiſes rung,
His ſonnets at the playhouſe ſung;
High waving o'er his lab'ring head,
The goddeſs Want her pinions ſpread,
And with poetic fury fir'd,
What Phœbus faintly had inſpir'd.
A noble Youth of taſte and wit,
Approv'd the ſprightly things he writ,

And

And ſought him in his cobweb dome,
Diſcharg'd his rent and brought him home.

Behold him at the ſtately board,
Who, but the Poet, and my Lord!
Each day deliciouſly he dines,
And greedy quaffs the generous wines;
His ſides were plump, his ſkin was ſleek,
And plenty wanton'd on his cheek;
Aſtoniſh'd at the change ſo new,
Away th' inſpiring goddeſs flew.

Now, dropt for politicks and news,
Neglected lay the drooping muſe,
Unmindful whence his fortune came,
He ſtifled the poetic flame;
Nor tale, nor ſonnet, for my lady,
Lampoon, nor epigram was ready.

With

With juſt contempt his patron ſaw,
(Reſolv'd his bounty to withdraw)
And thus, with anger in his look,
The late repenting fool beſpoke.

Blind to the good that courts thee grown,
Whence has the ſun of favour ſhone?
Delighted with thy tuneful art,
Eſteem was growing in my heart,
But idly thou reject'ſt the charm
That gave it birth, and kept it warm.

Unthinking fools, alone deſpiſe
The arts, that taught them firſt to riſe.

F. Hayman Inv. et delin. C. Mosley Sculp.

FABLE VI.

The Wolf, *the* Sheep, *and the* Lamb.

DUTY demands, the parent's voice
Should ſanctify the daughter's choice;
In that is due obedience ſhewn;
To chuſe belongs to her alone.
May horror ſeize his midnight hour,
Who builds upon a parent's pow'r,
And claims, by purchaſe vile and baſe,
The loathing maid for his embrace;

Hence virtue ſickens; and the breaſt,
Where peace had built her downy neſt,
Becomes the troubled ſeat of care,
And pines with anguiſh, and deſpair.

A Wolf, rapacious, rough and bold,
Whoſe nightly plunders thin'd the fold,
Contemplating his ill-ſpent life,
And cloy'd with thefts, would take a wife.
His purpoſe known, the ſavage race,
In num'rous crowds, attend the place;
For why, a mighty Wolf he was,
And held dominion in his jaws.
Her fav'rite whelp each mother brought,
And humbly his alliance ſought;

But

But cold by age, or elſe too nice,
None found acceptance in his eyes.
 It happen'd, as at early dawn
He ſolitary croſs'd the lawn,
Stray'd from the fold, a ſportive Lamb
Skip'd wanton by her fleecy Dam;
When Cupid, foe to man and beaſt,
Diſcharg'd an arrow at his breaſt.
 The tim'rous breed the robber knew,
And trembling o'er the meadow flew,
Their nimbleſt ſpeed the Wolf o'ertook,
And courteous, thus the Dam beſpoke.
Stay, faireſt, and ſuſpend your fear,
Truſt me, no enemy is near;
Theſe jaws, in ſlaughter oft imbru'd,
At length have known enough of blood;

And kinder bus'neſs brings me now,
Vanquiſh'd, at beauty's feet to bow.
You have a daughter———Sweet, forgive
A Wolf's addreſs———In her I live;
Love from her eyes like light'ning came,
And ſet my marrow all on flame;
Let your conſent confirm my choice,
And ratify our nuptial joys.

Me ample wealth, and pow'r attend,
Wide o'er the plains my realms extend;
What midnight robber dare invade
The fold, if I the guard am made?
At home the ſhepherd's curr may ſleep,
[illegible] ſecure his maſter's ſheep.
[illegible] courſe like this, attention claim'd;
[illegible] ndour the mother's breaſt inflam'd;

Now

Now fearlefs by his fide fhe walk'd,
Of fettlements and jointures talk'd;
Propos'd, and doubled her demands
Of flow'ry fields, and turnip-lands.
The Wolf agrees. Her bofom fwells;
To Mifs her happy fate fhe tells;
And of the grand alliance vain,
Contemns her kindred of the plain.

The loathing Lamb with horror hears,
And wearies out her Dam with pray'rs;
But all in vain; mamma beft knew
What unexperienc'd girls fhould do;
So, to the neighb'ring meadow carry'd,
A formal afs the couple marry'd.

Torn from the tyrant-mother's fide,
The trembler goes, a victim-bride,

Reluctant, meets the rude embrace,
And bleats among the howling race.
With horror oft her eyes behold
Her murder'd kindred of the fold;
Each day a sister-lamb is serv'd,
And at the Glutton's table carv'd;
The crashing bones he grinds for food,
And slakes his thirst with streaming blood.
Love, who the cruel mind detests,
And lodges but in gentle breasts,
Was now no more. Enjoyment past,
The savage hunger'd for the feast;
But (as we find in human race,
A mask conceals the villain's face)
Justice must authorize the treat;
Till then he long'd, but durst not eat.

As forth he walk'd, in queſt of prey,
The hunters met him on the way;
Fear wings his flight; the marſh he ſought;
The ſnuffing dogs are ſet at fault.
His ſtomach baulk'd, now hunger gnaws,
Howling, he grinds his empty jaws;
Food muſt be had, and lamb is nigh;
His maw invokes the fraudful lie.
Is this (diſſembling rage, he cry'd)
The gentle virtue of a bride?
That, leagu'd with man's deſtroying race,
She ſets her huſband for the chace?
By treach'ry prompts the noiſy hound
To ſcent his footſteps on the ground?
Thou trait'reſs vile! for this thy blood
Shall glut my rage, and dye the wood!

So ſaying, on the Lamb he flies,
Beneath his jaws the victim dies.

F. Hayman inv.t et delin: C. Mosley sculp

FABLE VII.

The GOOSE, *and the* SWANS.

I HATE the face, however fair,
That carries an affected air;
The liſping tone, the ſhape conſtrain'd,
The ſtudy'd look, the paſſion feign'd,
Are fopperies, which only tend
To injure what they ſtrive to mend.
With what ſuperior grace enchants
The face, which nature's pencil paints!

Where eyes, unexercis'd in art,
Glow with the meaning of the heart!
Where freedom, and good-humour ſit,
And eaſy gaiety, and wit!
Though perfect beauty be not there,
The maſter lines, the finiſh'd air,
We catch from every look delight,
And grow enamour'd at the ſight:
For beauty, though we all approve,
Excites our wonder, more than love;
While the agreeable ſtrikes ſure,
And gives the wounds we cannot cure.

Why then, my Amoret, this care
That forms you, in effect, leſs fair?
If nature on your cheek beſtows
A bloom, that emulates the roſe,

Or from ſome heav'nly image drew
A form, Apelles never knew,
Your ill-judg'd aid will you impart,
And ſpoil by meretricious art?
Or had you, nature's error, come
Abortive from the mother's womb,
Your forming care ſhe ſtill rejects,
Which only heightens her defects.
When ſuch, of glitt'ring jewels proud,
Still preſs the foremoſt in the croud,
At ev'ry public ſhew are ſeen,
With look awry, and aukward mein,
The gaudy dreſs attracts the eye,
And magnifies deformity.
  Nature may underdo her part,
But ſeldom wants the help of art;

Truſt

Truſt her, ſhe is your ſureſt friend,
Nor made your form for you to mend.

A Gooſe, affected, empty, vain,
The ſhrilleſt of the cackling train,
With proud, and elevated creſt,
Precedence claim'd above the reſt.
  Says ſhe, I laugh at human race,
Who ſay, geeſe hobble in their pace;
Look here!——the ſland'rous lie detect;
Not haughty man is ſo erect.
That peacock yonder! lord, how vain
The creature's of his gaudy train!
If both were ſtript, I'd pawn my word,
A gooſe would be the finer bird.

Nature, to hide her own defects,
Her bungled work with finery decks;
Were geeſe ſet off with half that ſhow,
Would men admire the peacock? No.

Thus vaunting croſs the mead ſhe ſtalks,
The cackling breed attend her walks;
The ſun ſhot down his noon-tide beams,
The Swans were ſporting in the ſtreams;
Their ſnowy plumes, and ſtately pride
Provok'd her ſpleen. Why there, ſhe cry'd,
Again, what arrogance we ſee!——
Thoſe creatures! how they mimic me!
Shall ev'ry fowl the waters ſkim,
Becauſe we geeſe are known to ſwim!
Humility they ſoon ſhall learn,
And their own emptineſs diſcern.

So

So, ſaying, with extended wings,
Lightly upon the wave ſhe ſprings;
Her boſom ſwells, ſhe ſpreads her plumes,
And the ſwan's ſtately creſt aſſumes.
Contempt and mockery enſu'd,
And burſts of laughter ſhook the flood.
A ſwan, ſuperior to the reſt,
Sprung forth, and thus the fool addreſs'd.
Conceited thing, elate with pride!
Thy affectation all deride;
Theſe airs thy aukwardneſs impart,
And ſhew thee plainly, as thou art.
Among thy equals of the flock,
Thou had'ſt eſcap'd the public mock,
And as thy parts to good conduce,
Been deem'd an honeſt, hobbling gooſe.

Learn hence, to ſtudy wiſdom's rules;
Know, foppery's the pride of fools;
And ſtriving nature to conceal,
You only her defects reveal.

Tab. 8.

FABLE VIII.

The LAWYER *and* JUSTICE.

LOVE! thou divineſt good below,
Thy pure delights few mortals know!
Our rebel hearts thy ſway diſown,
While tyrant luſt uſurps thy throne.
 The bounteous God of nature made
The ſexes for each other's aid,
Their mutual talents to employ,
To leſſen ills, and heighten joy.

To weaker woman he aſſign'd
That ſoft'ning gentleneſs of mind,
That can, by ſimpathy, impart
It's likeneſs, to the rougheſt heart.
Her eyes with magic pow'r endu'd,
To fire the dull, and awe the rude.
His roſy fingers on her face
Shed laviſh ev'ry blooming grace,
And ſtamp'd (perfection to diſplay)
His mildeſt image on her clay
  Man, active, reſolute, and bold,
He faſhion'd in a different mould,
With uſeful arts his mind inform'd,
His breaſt with nobler paſſions warm'd;
He gave him knowledge, taſte, and ſenſe,
And courage, for the fair's defence.

He

Her frame, reſiſtleſs to each wrong,
Demands protection from the ſtrong;
To man ſhe flies, when fear alarms,
And claims the temple of his arms.

By nature's author thus declar'd
The woman's ſovereign, and her guard,
Shall man, by treach'rous wiles invade
The weakneſs, he was meant to aid?
While beauty, given to inſpire
Protecting love, and ſoft deſire,
Lights up a wild-fire in the heart,
And to it's own breaſt points the dart,
Becomes the ſpoiler's baſe pretence
To triumph over innocence.

The Wolf, that tears the tim'rous ſheep,
Was never ſet the fold to keep;

Nor was the tyger, or the pard,
Meant the benighted trav'ller's guard;
But man, the wildeſt beaſt of prey,
Wears friendſhip's ſemblance to betray;
His ſtrength againſt the weak employs,
And where he ſhould protect, deſtroys.

PAST twelve o'clock, the watchman cry'd,
His brief the ſtudious Lawyer ply'd;
The all-prevailing fee lay nigh,
The earneſt of to-morrow's lie.
Sudden the furious winds ariſe,
The jarring caſement ſhatter'd flies;
The doors admit a hollow ſound,
And rattling from their hinges bound;

Whne

When Juſtice, in a blaze of light,
Reveal'd her radiant form to ſight.
  The wretch with thrilling horror ſhook,
Looſe every joint, and pale his look;
Not having ſeen her in the courts,
Or found her mention'd in reports,
He aſk'd, with fault'ring tongue, her name,
Her errand there, and whence ſhe came?
  Sternly the white-rob'd ſhade reply'd,
(A crimſon glow her viſage dy'd)
Can'ſt thou be doubtful who I am?
Is Juſtice grown ſo ſtrange a name?
Were not your courts for Juſtice rais'd?
'Twas there, of old, my altars blaz'd.
My guardian thee I did elect,
My ſacred temple to protect,

That thou, and all thy venal tribe
Should ſpurn the goddeſs for the bribe.
Aloud the ruin'd client cries,
Juſtice has neither ears, nor eyes;
In foul alliance with the bar,
'Gainſt me the judge denounces war,
And rarely iſſues his decree,
But with intent to baffle me.

She paus'd. Her breaſt with fury burn'd.
The trembling Lawyer thus return'd.

I own the charge is juſtly laid,
And weak th' excuſe that can be made;
Yet ſearch the ſpacious globe, and ſee
If all mankind are not like me.

The gown-man, ſkill'd in romiſh lies,
By faith's falſe glaſs deludes our eyes;

O'er

O'er confcience rides without controul,
And robs the man, to fave his foul.
  The Doctor, with important face,
By fly defign, miftakes the cafe;
Prefcribes and fpins out the difeafe,
To trick the patient of his fees.
  The foldier, rough with many a fcar,
And red with flaughter, leads the war;
If he a nation's truft betray,
The foe has offer'd double pay.
  When vice o'er all mankind prevails,
And weighty int'reft turns the fcales,
Muft I be better than the reft,
And harbour Juftice in my breaft?
On one fide only take the fee,
Content with poverty and thee?

Thou blind to ſenſe, and vile of mind,
Th' exaſperated Shade rejoin'd,
If virtue from the world is flown,
Will others faults excuſe thy own?
For ſickly ſouls the prieſt was made;
Phyſicians for the body's aid;
The ſoldier guarded liberty;
Man, woman, and the lawyer me.
If all are faithleſs to their truſt,
They leave not thee the leſs unjuſt.
Henceforth your pleadings I diſclaim,
And bar the ſanction of my name;
Within your courts it ſhall be read,
That Juſtice from the law is fled.
She ſpoke; and hid in ſhades her face,
'Till HARDWICK ſooth'd her into grace.

FABLE

Fable

FABLE IX.

The FARMER, *the* SPANIEL, *and the* CAT.

WHY knits my dear her angry brow?
What rude offence alarms you now?
I ſaid, that Delia's fair, 'tis true,
But did I ſay ſhe equall'd you?
Can't I another's face commend,
Or to her virtues be a friend,
But inſtantly your forehead lours,
As if her merit leſſen'd yours?

From ſemale envy never free,
All muſt be blind becauſe you ſee.

Survey the gardens, fields, and bow'rs,
The buds, the bloſſoms, and the flow'rs.
Then tell me where the wood-bine grows,
That vies in ſweetneſs with the roſe?
Or where the lilly's ſnowy white,
That throws ſuch beauties on the ſight?
Yet folly is it to declare,
That theſe are neither ſweet, nor fair.
The cryſtal ſhines with fainter rays,
Before the di'monds brighter blaze;
And fops will ſay, the di'mond dies
Before the luſtre of your eyes:
But I, who deal in truth, deny
That neither ſhine when you are by.

When

When zephirs o'er the bloſſoms ſtray,
And ſweets along the air convey,
Shan't I the fragrant breeze inhale,
Becauſe you breathe a ſweeter gale?
Sweet are the flow'rs that deck the field;
Sweet is the ſmell the bloſſoms yield;
Sweet is the ſummer gale that blows;
And ſweet, tho' ſweeter you, the roſe.
Shall envy then torment your breaſt,
If you are lovelier than the reſt?
For while I give to each her due,
By praiſing them I flatter you;
And praiſing moſt, I ſtill declare
You faireſt, where the reſt are fair.

AS at his board a farmer ſate,
Repleniſh'd by his homely treat,

His

His fav'rite Spaniel near him ſtood,
And with his maſter ſhar'd the food;
The crackling bones his jaws devour'd,
His lapping tongue the trenchers ſcour'd;
Till ſated now, ſupine he lay,
And ſnor'd the riſing fumes away.

The hungry Cat, in turn, drew near,
And humbly crav'd a ſervant's ſhare;
Her modeſt worth the Maſter knew,
And ſtrait the fat'ning morſel threw:
Enrag'd, the ſnarling cur awoke,
And thus with ſpiteful envy, ſpoke.

They only claim a right to eat,
Who earn by ſervices their meat;
Me, zeal and induſtry enflame
To ſcour the fields, and ſpring the game;

Or

Or, plunged in the wintry wave,
For man the wounded bird to ſave.
With watchful diligence I keep,
From prowling wolves, his fleecy ſheep;
At home his midnight hours ſecure,
And drive the robber from the door.
For this, his breaſt with kindneſs glows;
For this, his hand the food beſtows;
And ſhall thy indolence impart
A warmer friendſhip to his heart,
That thus he robs me of my due,
To pamper ſuch vile things as you?
I own (with meekneſs Puſs reply'd)
Superiour merit on your ſide;
Nor does my breaſt with envy ſwell,
To find it recompenc'd ſo well;

Yet

Yet I, in what my nature can,
Contribute to the good of man.
Whofe claws deftroy the pilf'ring moufe?
Who drives the vermin from the houfe?
Or, watchful for the lab'ring fwain,
From lurking rats fecure the grain?
From hence, if he rewards beftow,
Why fhould your heart with gall o'erflow?
Why pine my happinefs to fee,
Since there's enough for you and me?

Thy words are juft, the Farmer cry'd,
And fpurn'd the fnarler from his fide.

Tab. 10

FABLE X.

The Spider, *and the* Bee.

THE nymph, who walks the public
ſtreets,
And ſets her cap at all ſhe meets,
May catch the fool who turns to ſtare,
But men of ſenſe avoid the ſnare.

As on the margin of the flood,
With ſilken line, my Lydia ſtood,
I ſmil'd to ſee the pains you took,
To cover o'er the fraudful hook.

Along the foreſt as we ſtray'd,
You ſaw the boy his lime-twigs ſpread;
Gueſs'd you the reaſon of his fear,
Leſt, heedleſs, we approach'd too near?
For as behind the buſh we lay,
The linnet flutter'd on the ſpray.

Needs there ſuch caution to delude
The ſcaly fry, and feather'd brood?
And think you with inferior art,
To captivate the human heart?

The maid, who modeſtly conceals
Her beauties, while ſhe hides, reveals.
Give but a glimpſe, and fancy draws
Whate'er the Grecian Venus was.
From Eve's firſt fig-leaf to brocade,
All dreſs was meant for fancy's aid,

Which

Which evermore delighted dwells
On what the baſhful nymph conceals.

When Celia ſtruts in man's attire,
She ſhews too much to raiſe deſire;
But from the hoop's bewitching round,
Her very ſhoe has pow'r to wound.

The roving eye, the boſom bare,
The forward laugh, the wanton air,
May catch the fop; for gudgeons ſtrike
At the bare hook, and bait, alike;
While ſalmon play regardleſs by,
Till art, like nature, forms the fly.

BENEATH a peaſant's homely thatch,
A Spider long had held her watch;
From morn to night, with reſtleſs care,
She ſpun her web, and wove her ſnare.

Within the limits of her reign,
Lay many a heedleſs captive ſlain,
Or flutt'ring, ſtruggled in the toils,
To burſt the chains, and ſhun her wiles.

A ſtraying Bee, that perch'd hard by,
Beheld her with diſdainful eye,
And thus began. Mean thing, give o'er,
And lay thy ſlender threads no more;
A thoughtleſs fly or two, at moſt
Is all the conqueſt thou can'ſt boaſt;
For bees of ſenſe thy arts evade,
We ſee ſo plain the nets are laid.

The gaudy tulip, that diſplays
Her ſpreading foliage to gaze;
That points her charms at all ſhe ſees,
And yields to every wanton breeze.

Attracts not me; where blushing grows,
Guarded with thorns, the modest rose,
Enamour'd, round and round I fly,
Or on her fragrant bosom lie;
Reluctant, she my ardour meets,
And bashful, renders up her sweets.

To wiser heads attention lend,
And learn this lesson from a friend.
She, who with modesty retires,
Adds fewel to her lover's fires,
While such incautious jilts as you,
By folly your own schemes undo.

Fab.11.

F. Hayman inv. Grignion Sculp

FABLE XI.

The Young Lion *and the* Ape.

'TIS true, I blame your lover's choice,
Though flatter'd by the public voice,
And peevish grow, and sick, to hear
His exclamations, O how fair!
I listen not to wild delights,
And transports of expected nights;
What is to me your hoard of charms?
The whiteness of your neck and arms?
Needs there no acquisition more,
To keep contention from the door?

Yes; paſs a fortnight, and you'll find,
All beauty cloys, but of the mind.
  Senſe, and good-humour ever prove
The ſureſt cords to faſten love.
Yet, Phillis, ſimpleſt of your ſex,
You never think but to perplex;
Coquetting it with every ape,
That ſtruts abroad in human ſhape;
Not that the coxcomb is your taſte,
But that it ſting's your lover's breaſt;
To-morrow you reſign the ſway,
Prepar'd to honour and obey,
The tyrant-miſtreſs change for life,
To the ſubmiſſion of a wife.
  Your follies, if you can, ſuſpend,
And learn inſtruction from a friend.

Reluctant,

Reluctant, hear the firſt addreſs,
Think often, ere you anſwer, yes;
But once reſolv'd, throw off diſguiſe,
And wear your wiſhes in your eyes,
With caution ev'ry look forbear,
That might create one jealous fear,
A lover's ripening hopes confound,
Or give the gen'rous breaſt a wound.
Contemn the girliſh arts to teaze,
Nor uſe your pow'r, unleſs to pleaſe;
For fools alone with rigour ſway,
When ſoon, or late, they muſt obey.

THE king of brutes, in life's decline,
Reſolv'd dominion to reſign;

The beasts were summon'd to appear,
And bend before the royal heir.
They came; a day was fix'd; the crowd
Before their future monarch bow'd.

A dapper monkey, pert and vain,
Step'd forth, and thus address'd the train,
Why cringe my friends with slavish awe,
Before this pageant king of straw?
Shall we anticipate the hour,
And ere we feel it, own his pow'r?
The counsels of experience prize,
I know the maxims of the wise;
Subjection let us cast away,
And live the monarchs of to-day;
'Tis ours the vacant hand to spurn,
And play the tyrant each in turn.

So ſhall he right from wrong diſcern,
And mercy from oppreſſion learn;
At others woes be taught to melt,
And loath the ills himſelf has felt.
He ſpoke; his boſom ſwell'd with pride.
The youthful Lion thus reply'd.
What madneſs prompts thee to provoke
My wrath, and dare th' impending ſtroke?
Thou wretched fool! can wrongs impart
Compaſſion to the feeling heart?
Or teach the grateful breaſt to glow,
The hand to give, or eye to flow?
Learn'd in the practice of their ſchools,
From women thou haſt drawn thy rules;
To them return; in ſuch a cauſe,
From only ſuch expect applauſe;

The partial ſex I don't condemn,
For liking thoſe, who copy them.
  Would'ſt thou the gen'rous lion bind,
By kindneſs bribe him to be kind;
Good offices their likeneſs get,
And payment leſſens not the debt;
With multiplying hand he gives
The good, from others he receives;
Or, for the bad makes fair return,
And pays with int'reſt, ſcorn for ſcorn.

FABLE

Tab. 12.

F Hayman inv. C Grignion Sculp

FABLE XII.

The COLT, *and the* FARMER.

TELL me, Corinna, if you can,
Why ſo averſe, ſo coy to man?
Did nature, laviſh of her care,
From her beſt pattern form you fair,
That you, ungrateful to her cauſe,
Should mock her gifts, and ſpurn her laws?
And, miſer-like, with-hold that ſtore,
Which, by imparting, bleſſes more?

Beauty's a gift, by heaven aſſign'd
The portion of the female kind;
For this the yielding maid demands
Protection at her lover's hands;
And though by waſting years it fade,
Remembrance tells him, once 'twas paid.

And will you then this wealth conceal,
For age to ruſt, or time to ſteal?
The ſummer of your youth to rove,
A ſtranger to the joys of love?
Then, when life's winter haſtens on,
And youth's fair heritage is gone,
Dow'rleſs to court ſome peaſant's arms,
To guard your wither'd age from harms,
No gratitude to warm his breaſt,
For blooming beauty once poſſeſs'd;

How

How will you curſe that ſtubborn pride,
Which drove your bark acroſs the tide,
And ſailing before folly's wind,
Left ſenſe and happineſs behind?
Corinna, leſt theſe whims prevail,
To ſuch as you, I write my tale.

A Colt, for blood, and mettled ſpeed,
The choiceſt of the running breed,
Of youthful ſtrength, and beauty vain,
Refus'd ſubjection to the rein.
In vain the groom's officious ſkill
Oppos'd his pride, and check'd his will;
In vain the maſter's forming care
Reſtrain'd with threats, or ſooth'd with pray'r;

Of freedom proud, and ſcorning man,
Wild o'er the ſpacious plains he ran.

Where e'er luxuriant nature ſpread
Her flow'ry carpet o'er the mead,
Or bubbling ſtreams ſoft-gliding paſs
To cool and freſhen up the graſs,
Diſdaining bounds, he cropt the blade,
And wanton'd in the ſpoil he made.

In plenty thus the ſummer paſs'd,
Revolving winter came at laſt;
The trees no more a ſhelter yield,
The verdure withers from the field,
Perpetual ſnows inveſt the ground,
In icy chains the ſtreams are bound,
Cold, nipping winds, and rattling hail,
His lank, unſhelter'd ſides aſſail.

As

As round he caſt his rueful eyes,
He ſaw the thatch'd-roof cottage riſe;
The proſpect touch'd his heart with chear;
And promis'd kind deliv'rance near.
A ſtable, erſt his ſcorn and hate,
Was now become his wiſh'd retreat;
His paſſion cool, his pride forgot,
A Farmer's welcome yard he ſought.

The maſter ſaw his woeful plight,
His limbs that totter'd with his weight,
And, friendly, to the ſtable led,
And ſaw him litter'd, dreſs'd, and fed.
In ſlothful eaſe, all night he lay;
The ſervants roſe at break of day;
The market calls. Along the road,
His back muſt bear the pond'rous load;

In vain he ſtruggles, or complains,
Inceſſant blows reward his pains.
To-morrow varies but his toil;
Chain'd to the plough, he breaks the ſoil;
While ſcanty meals at night repay
The painful labours of the day.

Subdu'd by toil, with anguiſh rent,
His ſelf-upbraidings found a vent.
Wretch that I am! he ſighing ſaid,
By arrogance and folly led,
Had but my reſtive youth been brought
To learn the leſſon nature taught,
Then had I, like my ſires of yore,
The prize from every courſer bore;
While man beſtow'd rewards and praiſe,
And females crown'd my latter days.

Now

Now lasting servitude's my lot,
My birth contemn'd, my speed forgot,
Doom'd am I, for my pride, to bear
A living death, from year to year.

F. Hayman inv. et del. C. Mosley sculp.

FABLE XIII.

The Owl, *and the* Nightingale.

TO know the miſtreſs' humour right,
See if her maids are clean and tight;
If Betty waits without her ſtays,
She copies but her lady's ways.
When Miſs comes in with boiſt'rous ſhout,
And drops no curt'ſy, going out,
Depend upon't, mamma is one,
Who reads, or drinks too much alone.

If bottled beer her thirſt aſſwage,
She feels enthuſiaſtic rage,
And burns with ardour to inherit
The gifts, and workings of the ſpirit.
If learning crack her giddy brains,
No remedy, but death remains.
Sum up the various ills of life,
And all are ſweet, to ſuch a wife.
At home, ſuperior wit ſhe vaunts,
And twits her huſband with his wants;
Her ragged offspring all around,
Like pigs, are wallowing on the ground;
Impatient ever of controul,
She knows no order, but of ſoul;
With books her litter'd floor is ſpread,
Of nameleſs authors, never read;

Foul

Foul linen, petticoats, and lace
Fill up the intermediate ſpace.
Abroad, at viſitings, her tongue
Is never ſtill, and always wrong;
All meanings ſhe defines away,
And ſtands, with truth and ſenſe, at bay.
  If e'er ſhe meets a gentle heart,
Skill'd in the houſewife's uſeful art,
Who makes her family her care,
And builds contentment's temple there,
She ſtarts at ſuch miſtakes in nature,
And cries, lord help us!—what a creature!
  Meliſſa, if the moral ſtrike,
You'll find the fable not unlike.
  An Owl, puff'd up with ſelf-conceit,
Lov'd learning better than his meat;

Old manuſcripts he treaſur'd up,
And rummag'd every grocer's ſhop;
At paſtry-cooks was known to ply,
And ſtrip, for ſcience, every pye.
For modern poetry, and wit,
He had read all that Blackmore writ;
So intimate with Curl was grown,
His learned treaſures were his own;
To all his authors had acceſs,
And ſometimes would correct the preſs.
In logic he acquir'd ſuch knowledge,
You'd ſwear him fellow of a college;
Alike to every art, and ſcience,
His daring genius bid defiance,
And ſwallow'd wiſdom, with that haſte,
That cits do cuſtards at a feaſt.

Within the ſhelter of a wood,
One ev'ning, as he muſing ſtood,
Hard by, upon a leafy ſpray,
A Nightingale began his lay.
Sudden he ſtarts, with anger ſtung,
And ſcreeching interrupts the ſong.

Pert, buſy thing, thy airs give o'er,
And let my contemplations ſoar.
What is the muſic of thy voice,
But jarring diſſonance, and noiſe?
Be wiſe. True harmony, thou'lt find,
Not in the throat, but in the mind;
By empty chirping not attain'd,
But by laborious ſtudy gain'd.
Go, read the authors Pope explodes,
Fathom the depth of Cibber's odes,

With modern plays improve thy wit,
Read all the learning Henley writ;
And if thou needs muſt ſing, ſing then,
And emulate the ways of men;
So ſhalt thou grow, like me refin'd,
And bring improvement to thy kind.

Thou wretch, the little Warbler cry'd,
Made up of ignorance, and pride,
Aſk all the birds, and they'll declare,
A greater blockhead wings not air.
Read o'er thyſelf, thy talents ſcan,
Science was only meant for man.
No ſenſeleſs authors me moleſt,
I mind the duties of my neſt;
With careful wing, protect my young,
And chear their ev'nings with a ſong;

Make

Make ſhort the weary trav'ller's way,
And warble in the poet's lay.

Thus, following nature, and her laws,
From men, and birds I claim applauſe;
While, nurs'd in pedantry and ſloth,
An Owl is ſcorn'd alike by both.

Fable 14

F Hayman inv · C Grignion Sculp

FABLE XIV.

The SPARROW, *and the* DOVE.

IT was, as learn'd traditions ſay,
Upon an April's blithſome day,
When pleaſure, ever on the wing,
Return'd, companion of the ſpring,
And chear'd the birds with am'rous heat,
Inſtructing little hearts to beat;
A ſparrow, frolic, gay, and young,
Of bold addreſs, and flippant tongue,

Juſt

Juſt left his lady of a night,
Like him, to follow new delight.
The youth, of many a conqueſt vain,
Flew off to ſeek the chirping train;
The chirping train he quickly found,
And with a ſaucy eaſe, bow'd round.
For every ſhe his boſom burns,
And this, and that he wooes by turns;
And here a ſigh, and there a bill,
And here—thoſe eyes, ſo form'd to kill!
And now with ready tongue, he ſtrings
Unmeaning, ſoft, reſiſtleſs things;
With vows, and dem-me's ſkill'd to woo
As other pretty fellows do.
Not that he thought this ſhort eſſay
A prologue needful to his play;

No,

No, truſt me, ſays our learned letter,
He knew the virtuous ſex much better;
But theſe he held as ſpecious arts,
To ſhew his own ſuperior parts,
The form of decency to ſhield,
And give a juſt pretence to yield.

Thus finiſhing his courtly play,
He mark'd the fav'rite of a day;
With careleſs impudence drew near,
And whiſper'd hebrew in her ear;
A hint, which like the maſon's ſign,
The conſcious can alone divine.

The flutt'ring nymph, expert at feigning,
Cry'd, Sir!--pray Sir, explain your meaning--
Go prate to thoſe, that may endure ye—
To me this rudeneſs!—I'll aſſure ye!——

Then off ſhe glided, like a ſwallow,
As ſaying——you gueſs where to follow.
  To ſuch as know the party ſet,
'Tis needleſs to declare they met;
The parſon's barn, as authors mention,
Confeſs'd the fair had apprehenſion.
Her honour there ſecure from ſtain,
She held all farther trifling vain,
No more affected to be coy,
But ruſh'd licentious, on the joy.
  Hiſt, love!—the male companion cry'd,
Retire a while, I fear we're ſpy'd.
Nor was the caution vain; he ſaw
A Turtle, ruſtling in the ſtraw,
While o'er her callow brood ſhe hung,
And fondly thus addreſs'd her young.

Ye tender objects of my care!
Peace, peace, ye little helpless pair;
Anon he comes, your gentle sire,
And brings you all your hearts require.
For us, his infants, and his bribe,
For us, with only love to guide,
Our lord assumes an eagle's speed,
And like a lion, dares to bleed.
Nor yet by wint'ry skies confin'd,
He mounts upon the rudest wind,
From danger tears the vital spoil,
And with affection sweetens toil.
Ah cease, too vent'rous! cease to dare,
In thine, our dearer safety spare!
From him, ye cruel falcons, stray,
And turn, ye fowlers, far away!

Should I ſurvive to ſee the day,
That tears me from myſelf away,
That cancels all that heav'n could give,
The life, by which alone I live,
Alas, how more than loſt were I,
Who, in the thought, already die!

Ye pow'rs, whom men, and birds obey,
Great rulers of your creatures, ſay,
Why mourning comes, by bliſs convey'd,
And ev'n the ſweets of love allay'd?
Where grows enjoyment, tall, and fair,
Around it twines entangling care;
While fear for what our ſouls poſſeſs,
Enervates every pow'r to bleſs;
Yet friendſhip forms the bliſs above,
And, life! what art thou, without love?

Our

Our hero, who had heard apart,
Felt ſomething moving in his heart,
But quickly, with diſdain, ſuppreſs'd
The virtue, riſing in his breaſt;
And firſt he feign'd to laugh aloud,
And next, approaching, ſmil'd and bow'd.

Madam, you muſt not think me rude;
Good manners never can intrude;
I vow I come thro' pure good nature—
(Upon my ſoul a charming creature)
Are theſe the comforts of a wife?
This careful, cloiſtered, moaping life?
No doubt, that odious thing, call'd duty,
Is a ſweet province for a beauty.
Thou pretty ignorance! thy will
Is meaſur'd to thy want of ſkill;

That good old-faſhion'd dame, thy mother,
Has taught thy infant years no other—
The greateſt ill in the creation,
Is ſure the want of education.

But think ye?—tell me without feigning,
Have all theſe charms no farther meaning?
Dame nature, if you don't forget her,
Might teach your ladyſhip much better.
For ſhame, reject this mean employment,
Enter the world, and taſte enjoyment;
Where time, by circling bliſs, we meaſure;
Beauty was form'd alone for pleaſure;
Come, prove the bleſſing, follow me,
Be wiſe, be happy, and be free.

Kind Sir, reply'd our matron chaſte,
Your zeal ſeems pretty much in haſte;

I own

I own, the fondneſs to be bleſs'd
Is a deep thirſt in every breaſt;
Of bleſſings too I have my ſtore,
Yet quarrel not, ſhould heav'n give more;
Then prove the change to be expedient,
And think me, Sir, your moſt obedient.

Here turning, as to one inferior,
Our gallant ſpoke, and ſmil'd ſuperior.
Methinks, to quit your boaſted ſtation
Requires a world of heſitation;
Where brats, and bonds are held a bleſſing,
The caſe, I doubt, is paſt redreſſing.
Why, child, ſuppoſe the joys I mention,
Were the mere fruits of my invention,
You've cauſe ſufficient for your carriage,
In flying from the curſe of marriage;

That ſly decoy, with vary'd ſnares,
That takes your widgeons in by pairs;
Alike to huſband, and to wife,
The cure of love, and bane of life;
The only method of forecaſting,
To make misfortune firm, and laſting;
The ſin, by heav'n's peculiar ſentence,
Unpardon'd, through a life's repentance.
It is the double ſnake, that weds
A common tail to diff'rent heads,
That lead the carcaſs ſtill aſtray,
By dragging each a diff'rent way.
Of all the ills, that may attend me,
From marriage, mighty gods, defend me!

Give Me frank nature's wild demeſnee,
And boundleſs tract of air ſerene,

Where

Where fancy, ever wing'd for change,
Delights to ſport, delights to range;
There, Liberty! to thee is owing
Whate'er of bliſs is worth beſtowing;
Delights, ſtill vary'd, and divine,
Sweet goddeſs of the hills! are thine.

What ſay you now, you pretty pink you?
Have I, for once ſpoke reaſon, think you?
You take me now for no romancer—
Come, never ſtudy for an anſwer;
Away, caſt every care behind ye,
And fly where joy alone ſhall find ye.

Soft yet, return'd our female fencer,
A queſtion more, or ſo——and then, Sir.
You've rally'd me with ſenſe exceeding,
With much fine wit, and better breeding;

But pray, Sir, how do You contrive it?
Do thofe of your world never wive it?
" No, no," How then? " Why, dare I tell,
" What does the bus'nefs full as well."
Do you ne'er love? " An hour at leifure."
Have you no friendfhips? " Yes, for pleafure."
No care for little ones? " We get 'em,
" The reft the mothers mind, and let 'em."

Thou wretch, rejoin'd the kindling Dove,
Quite loft to life, as loft to love!
When'er misfortune comes, how juft!
And come misfortune furely muft;
In the dread feafon of difmay,
In that, your hour of trial, fay,
Who then fhall prop your finking heart?
Who bear affliction's weightier part?

Say

Say, when the black-brow'd welken bends,
And winter's gloomy form impends,
To mourning turns all tranſient chear,
And blaſts the melancholy year;
For times, at no perſuaſion, ſtay,
Nor vice can find perpetual May;
Then where's that tongue, by folly fed,
That ſoul of pertneſs, whither fled?
All ſhrunk within thy lonely neſt,
Forlorn, abandoned, and unbleſs'd;
No friends, by cordial bonds ally'd,
Shall ſeek thy cold, unſocial ſide;
No chirping prattlers, to delight
Shall turn the long-enduring night;
No bride her words of balm impart,
And warm thee at her conſtant heart.

Freedom, restrain'd by reason's force,
Is as the sun's unvarying course,
Benignly active, sweetly bright,
Affording warmth, affording light;
But torn from virtue's sacred rules,
Becomes a comet, gaz'd by fools,
Foreboding cares, and storms, and strife,
And fraught with all the plagues of life.

Thou fool! by union every creature
Subsists, through universal nature;
And this, to beings void of mind,
Is wedlock, of a meaner kind.

While womb'd in space, primæval clay
A yet unfashion'd embryo lay,
The source of endless good above
Shot down his spark of kindling love;

Touch'd by the all-enlivening flame,
Then motion first exulting came;
Each atom sought its seperate class,
Through many a fair, enamour'd mass;
Love cast the central charm around,
And with eternal nuptials bound.
Then form, and order o'er the sky,
First train'd their bridal pomp on high;
The sun display'd his orb to sight,
And burnt with hymeneal light.

Hence nature's virgin-womb conceiv'd,
And with the genial burden heav'd;
Forth came the oak, her first born heir
And scal'd the breathing steep of air;
Then infant stems of various use,
Imbib'd her soft, maternal juice;

The flow'rs, in early bloom disclos'd;
Upon her fragrant breast repos'd;
Within her warm embraces grew
A race of endless form, and hue;
Then pour'd her lesser offspring round,
And fondly cloath'd their parent ground.

Nor here alone the virtue reign'd,
By matter's cumb'ring form detain'd;
But thence, subliming, and refin'd,
Aspir'd, and reach'd its kindred Mind.
Caught in the fond, celestial fire,
The mind perceiv'd unknown desire,
And now with kind effusion flow'd,
And now with cordial ardours glow'd,
Beheld the sympathetic fair,
And lov'd its own resemblance there;

On all with circling radiance ſhone,
But cent'ring, fix'd on one alone;
There claſp'd the heav'n appointed wife,
And doubled every joy of life.

Here ever bleſſing, ever bleſs'd,
Reſides this beauty of the breaſt,
As from his palace, here the god
Still beams effulgent bliſs abroad,
Here gems his own eternal round,
The ring, by which the world is bound,
Here bids his ſeat of empire grow,
And builds his little heav'n below.

The bridal partners thus ally'd,
And thus in ſweet accordance ty'd,
One body, heart and ſpirit live,
Enrich'd by every joy they give;

Like

Like echo, from her vocal hold,
Return'd in music twenty fold.
Their union firm, and undecay'd,
Nor time can shake, nor pow'r invade,
But as the stem, and scion stand,
Ingrafted by a skilful hand,
They check the tempest's wintry rage,
And bloom and strengthen into age.
A thousand amities unknown,
And pow'rs, perceiv'd by love alone,
Endearing looks, and chaste desire,
Fan, and support the mutual fire,
Whose flame, perpetual, as refin'd,
Is fed by an immortal mind.

Nor yet the nuptial sanction ends,
Like Nile it opens, and descends,

Which, by apparent windings led,
We trace to its celeſtial head.
The fire, firſt ſpringing from above,
Becomes the ſource of life and love,
And gives his filial heir to flow,
In fondneſs down on ſons below:
Thus roll'd in one continu'd tide,
To time's extremeſt verge they glide,
While kindred ſtreams, on either hand,
Branch forth in bleſſings o'er the land.

Thee, wretch! no liſping babe ſhall name,
No late-returning brother claim,
No kinſman on thy road rejoice,
No ſiſter greet thy ent'ring voice,
With partial eyes no parents ſee,
And bleſs their years reſtor'd in thee.

In

In age rejected, or declin'd,
An alien, ev'n among thy kind,
The partner of thy ſcorn'd embrace,
Shall play the wanton in thy face,
Each ſpark unplume thy little pride,
All friendſhip fly thy faithleſs ſide,
Thy name ſhall like thy carcaſs rot,
In ſickneſs ſpurn'd, in death forgot.

All-giving pow'r! great ſource of life!
O hear the parent! hear the wife!
That life thou lendeſt from above,
Though little, make it large in love;
O bid my feeling heart expand
To ev'ry claim, on ev'ry hand;
To thoſe, from whom my days I drew,
To theſe, in whom thoſe days renew,

To all my kin, however wide,
In cordial warmth, as blood ally'd,
To friends, with ſteely fetters twin'd,
And to the cruel, not unkind!

But chief, the lord of my deſire,
My life, myſelf, my ſoul, my fire,
Friends, children, all that wiſh can claim,
Chaſte paſſion claſp, and rapture name;
O ſpare him, ſpare him, gracious pow'r!
O give him to my lateſt hour!
Let me my length of life employ,
To give my ſole enjoyment joy.
His love, let mutual love excite,
Turn all my cares to his delight,
And every needleſs bleſſing ſpare,
Wherein my darling wants a ſhare.

When

When he with graceful action wooes,
And ſweetly bills, and fondly cooes,
Ah! deck me, to his eyes alone,
With charms attractive as his own,
And in my circling wings careſs'd,
Give all the lover to my breaſt.
Then in our chaſte, connubial bed,
My boſom pillow'd for his head,
His eyes, with bliſsful ſlumbers cloſe,
And watch, with me, my lord's repoſe,
Your peace around his temples twine,
And love him, with a love like mine.

And, for I know his gen'rous flame,
Beyond whate'er my ſex can claim,
Me too to your protection take,
And ſpare me for my huſband's ſake.

 Let

Let one unruffled, calm delight,
The loving, and belov'd unite;
One pure desire our bosoms warm,
One will direct, one wish inform;
Through life, one mutual aid sustain,
In death, one peaceful grave contain.

While, swelling with the darling theme,
Her accents pour'd an endless stream,
The well-known wings a sound impart,
That reach'd her ear, and touch'd her heart;
Quick drop'd the music of her tongue,
And forth, with eager joy, she sprung.
As swift her ent'ring consort flew,
And plum'd, and kindled at the view;
Their wings their souls embracing meet,
Their hearts with answering measure beat;

Half

Half loſt in ſacred ſweets, and bleſs'd
With raptures felt, but ne'er expreſs'd.
Strait to her humble roof ſhe led
The partner of her ſpotleſs bed;
Her young, a flutt'ting pair, ariſe,
Their welcome ſparkling in their eyes;
Tranſported, to their ſire they bound,
And hang with ſpeechleſs action round.
In pleaſure wrapt, the parents ſtand,
And ſee their little wings expand;
The ſire, his life-ſuſtaining prize
To each expecting bill applies,
There fondly pours the wheaten ſpoil,
With tranſport giv'n, tho' won with toil;
While, all collected at the ſight,
And ſilent through ſupreme delight,

The

The fair high heav'n of bliſs beguiles,
And on her lord, and infants ſmiles.

The Sparrow, whoſe attention hung
Upon the Dove's enchanting tongue,
Of all his little ſlights diſarm'd,
And from himſelf, by virtue, charm'd,
When now he ſaw, what only ſeem'd,
A fact, ſo late a fable deem'd,
His ſoul to envy he reſign'd,
His hours of folly to the wind,
In ſecret wiſh'd a turtle too,
And ſighing to himſelf, withdrew.

Fab. XV.

F. Hayman inv. et del. S. F. Ravenet Sculp.

FABLE XV.

The FEMALE SEDUCERS.

'TIS ſaid of widow, maid and wife,
That honour is a woman's life;
Unhappy ſex! who only claim
A being, in the breath of fame,
Which tainted, not the quick'ning gales,
That ſweep Sabæa's ſpicy vales,
Nor all the healing ſweets reſtore,
That breathe along Arabia's ſhore.

The trav'ler, if he chance to ſtray,
May turn uncenſur'd to his way;
Polluted ſtreams again are pure,
And deepeſt wounds admit a cure;
But woman! no redemption knows,
The wounds of honour never cloſe.

Tho' diſtant ev'ry hand to guide,
Nor ſkill'd on life's tempeſtuous tide,
If once her feeble bark recede,
Or deviate from the courſe decreed,
In vain ſhe ſeeks the friendleſs ſhore,
Her ſwifter folly flies before;
The circling ports againſt her cloſe,
And ſhut the wand'rer from repoſe;
'Till, by conflicting waves oppreſs'd,
Her found'ring pinnance ſinks to reſt.

Are

Are there no off'rings to atone
For but a ſingle error?—None.
Tho' woman is avow'd, of old,
No daughter of celeſtial mold,
Her temp'ring not without allay,
And form'd but of the finer clay,
We challenge from the mortal dame
The ſtrength angelic natures claim;
Nay more; for ſacred ſtories tell,
That ev'n immortal angels fell.

Whatever fills the teeming ſphere
Of humid earth, and ambient air,
With varying elements endu'd,
Was form'd to fall, and riſe renew'd.

The ſtars no fix'd duration know,
Wide oceans ebb, again to flow,

The moon repletes her waining face,
All-beauteous, from her late disgrace,
And suns, that mourn approaching night,
Refulgent rise with new-born light.

In vain may death, and time subdue,
While nature mints her race anew,
And holds some vital spark apart,
Like virtue, hid in ev'ry heart;
'Tis hence reviving warmth is seen,
To cloathe a naked world in green.
No longer barr'd by winter's cold,
Again the gates of life unfold;
Again each insect tries his wing,
And lifts fresh pinions on the spring;
Again from every latent root
The bladed stem, and tendril shoot,

Exhaling incenſe to the ſkies,
Again to periſh, and to riſe.

And muſt weak woman then diſown
The change, to which a world is prone?
In one meridian brightneſs ſhine,
And ne'er like ev'ning ſuns decline?
Reſolv'd and firm alone?——Is this
What we demand of woman?——Yes.

But ſhould the ſpark of veſtal fire,
In ſome unguarded hour expire.
Or ſhould the nightly thief invade
Heſperia's chaſte, and ſacred ſhade,
Of all the blooming ſpoil poſſeſs'd,
The dragon honour charm'd to reſt,
Shall virtue's flame no more return?
No more with virgin ſplendor burn?

No more the ravag'd garden blow
With ſpring's ſucceeding bloſſom?—No.
Pity may mourn, but not reſtore,
And woman falls, to riſe no more.

WITHIN this ſublunary ſphere,
A country lies——no matter where;
The clime may readily be found
By all, who tread poetic ground,
A ſtream, call'd life, acroſs it glides,
And equally the land divides;
And here, of vice the province lies,
And there, the hills of virtue riſe.

Upon a mountain's airy ſtand,
Whoſe ſummit look'd to either land,

An

An antient pair their dwelling chose,
As well for prospect, as repose;
For mutual faith they long were fam'd,
And Temp'rance, and Religion, nam'd.

A num'rous progeny divine,
Confess'd the honours of their line;
But in a little daughter fair,
Was center'd more than half their care;
For heav'n, to gratulate her birth,
Gave signs of future joy to earth;
White was the robe this infant wore,
And Chastity the name she bore.

As now the maid in stature grew,
(A flow'r just opening to the view)
Oft thro' her native lawns she stray'd,
And wrestling with the lambkins play'd;

Her looks diffusive sweets bequeath'd,
The breeze grew purer as she breath'd,
The morn her radient blush assum'd,
The spring with earlier fragrance bloom'd,
And nature yearly took delight,
Like her, to dress the world in white.

But when her rising form was seen
To reach the crisis of fifteen,
Her parents up the mountain's head,
With anxious step their darling led;
By turns they snatch'd her to their breast,
And thus the fears of age express'd.

O! joyful cause of many a care!
O! daughter too divinely fair!
Yon world, on this important day,
Demands thee to a dang'rous way;

A painful

A painful journey, all muſt go,
Whoſe doubted period none can know,
Whoſe due direction who can find,
Where reaſon's mute, and ſenſe is blind?
Ah, what unequal leaders theſe,
Thro' ſuch a wide, perplexing maze!
Then mark the warnings of the wiſe,
And learn what love, and years adviſe.

Far to the right thy proſpect bend,
Where yonder tow'ring hills aſcend;
Lo, there the arduous paths in view,
Which virtue, and her ſons purſue;
With toil o'er leſs'ning earth they riſe,
And gain, and gain upon the ſkies.
Narrow's the way her children tread,
No walk, for pleaſure ſmoothly ſpread,

But rough, and difficult, and ſteep,
Painful to climb, and hard to keep.

Fruits immature thoſe lands diſpenſe,
A food indelicate to ſenſe,
Of taſte unpleaſant; yet from thoſe
Pure health, with chearful vigour flows,
And ſtrength, unfeeling of decay,
Throughout the long, laborious way.

Hence, as they ſcale that heav'nly road,
Each limb is lightened of its load;
From earth refining ſtill they go,
And leave the mortal weight below;
Then ſpreads the ſtrait, the doubtful clears,
And ſmooth the rugged path appears;
For cuſtom turns fatigue to eaſe,
And, taught by virtue, pain can pleaſe.

At

At length, the toilſome journey o'er,
And near the bright, celeſtial ſhore,
A gulph, black, fearful, and profound,
Appears, of either world the bound,
Thro' darkneſs, leading up to light;
Senſe backwards ſhrinks, and ſhuns the ſight;
For there the tranſitory train,
Of time, and form, and care, and pain,
And matter's groſs, incumb'ring maſs,
Man's late aſſociates, cannot paſs,
But ſinking, quit th' immortal charge,
And leave the wond'ring ſoul at large;
Lightly ſhe wings her obvious way,
And mingles with eternal day.

Thither, O thither wing thy ſpeed,
Tho' pleaſure charm, or pain impede;

To

To ſuch th' all-bounteous pow'r has giv'n,
For preſent earth, a future heav'n;
For trivial loſs, unmeaſur'd gain,
And endleſs bliſs, for tranſient pain.

Then fear, ah! fear to turn thy ſight,
Where yonder flow'ry fields invite;
Wide on the left the path-way bends,
And with pernicious eaſe deſcends;
There ſweet to ſenſe, and fair to ſhow,
New-planted Edens ſeem to blow,
Trees, that delicious poiſon bear,
For death is vegetable there.

Hence is the frame of health unbrac'd,
Each ſinew ſlack'ning at the taſte,
The ſoul to paſſion yields her throne,
And ſees with organs not her own;

While

While, like the ſlumb'rer in the night,
Pleas'd with the ſhadowy dream of light,
Before her alienated eyes,
The ſcenes of fairy-land ariſe;
The puppet world's amuſing ſhow,
Dipt in the gayly-colour'd bow,
Scepters, and wreaths, and glitt'ring things,
The toys of infants, and of kings,
That tempt, along the baneful plain,
The idly wiſe, and lightly vain,
Till verging on the gulphy ſhore,
Sudden they ſink, and riſe no more.

But liſt to what thy fates declare;
Tho' thou art woman, frail as fair,
If once thy ſliding foot ſhould ſtray,
Once quit yon heav'n-appointed way,

For

For thee, loſt maid, for thee alone,
Nor pray'rs ſhall plead, nor tears atone;
Reproach, ſcorn, infamy, and hate,
On thy returning ſteps ſhall wait,
Thy form be loath'd by every eye,
And every foot thy preſence fly.

Thus arm'd with words of potent ſound,
Like guardian-angels plac'd around,
A charm, by truth divinely caſt,
Forward, our young advent'rer paſs'd,
Forth from her ſacred eye-lids ſent,
Like morn, fore-running radience went,
While honour, hand-maid late aſſign'd,
Upheld her lucid train behind.

Awe-ſtruck the much admiring-crowd
Before the virgin viſion bow'd,

Gaz'd with an ever new delight,
And caught fresh virtue at the sight;
For not of earth's unequal frame
They deem the heav'n-compounded Dame;
If matter, sure the most refin'd,
High wrought, and temper'd into mind,
Some darling daughter of the day,
And body'd by her native ray.

Where-e'er she passes, thousands bend,
And thousands, where she moves, attend;
Her ways observant eyes confess,
Her steps pursuing praises bless;
While to the elevated Maid
Oblations, as to heav'n are paid.

'Twas on an ever blithsome day,
The jovial birth of rosy May,

When genial warmth, no more ſuppreſs'd,
New melts the froſt in ev'ry breaſt,
The cheek with ſecret fluſhing dies;
And looks kind things from chaſteſt eyes;
The ſun with healthier viſage glows,
Aſide his clouded kerchief throws,
And dances up th' etherial plain,
Where late he us'd to climb with pain,
While nature, as from bonds ſet free
Springs out, and gives a looſe to glee.

And now for momentary reſt,
The nymph her travell'd ſtep repreſs'd,
Juſt turn'd to view the ſtage attain'd,
And glory'd in the height ſhe gain'd.

Out-ſtretch'd before her wide ſurvey,
The realms of ſweet perdition lay,

And pity touch'd her ſoul with woe,
To ſee a world ſo loſt below;
When ſtrait the breeze began to breathe
Airs, gently wafted from beneath,
That bore commiſſion'd witchcraft thence,
And reach'd her ſympathy of ſenſe;
No ſounds of diſcord, that diſcloſe
A people ſunk and loſt in woes,
But as of preſent good poſſeſs'd,
The very triumph of the bleſs'd.
The maid in rapt attention hung,
While thus approaching Sirens ſung.

Hither, faireſt, hither haſte,
Brighteſt beauty, come and taſte
What the pow'rs of bliſs unfold,
Joys, too mighty to be told;

Taste what extasies they give,
Dying raptures taste and live.

In thy lap, disdaining measure,
Nature empties all her treasure,
Soft desires, that sweetly languish,
Fierce delights, that rise to anguish;
Fairest, dost thou yet delay?
Brightest beauty, come away.

List not, when the froward chide,
Sons of pedantry, and pride,
Snarlers, to whose feeble sense
April's sunshine is offence;
Age and envy will advise
Ev'n against the joy they prize.

Come, in pleasure's balmly bowl,
Slake the thirstings of thy soul,

Till

Till thy raptur'd pow'rs are fainting
With enjoyment, paſt the painting;
Faireſt, do thou yet delay?
Brighteſt beauty, come away.

So ſung the Sirens, as of yore,
Upon the falſe Auſonian ſhore;
And O! for that preventing chain,
That bound Ulyſſes on the main,
That ſo our Fair One might withſtand
The covert ruin, now at hand.

The ſong her charm'd attention drew,
When now the tempters ſtood in view;
Curioſity, with prying eyes,
And hands of buſy, bold empriſe;
Like Hermes, feather'd were her feet,
And, like fore-running fancy, fleet.

By ſearch untaught, by toil untir'd,
To novelty ſhe ſtill aſpir'd,
Taſteleſs of ev'ry good poſſeſs'd,
And but in expectation bleſs'd.

With her, aſſociate, Pleaſure came,
Gay Pleaſure, frolic-loving dame,
Her mein, all ſwimming in delight,
Her beauties half reveal'd to ſight;
Looſe flow'd her garments from the ground,
And caught the kiſſing wings around.
As erſt Meduſa's looks were known
To turn beholders into ſtone,
A dire reverſion here they felt,
And in the eye of Pleaſure melt.
Her glance with ſweet perſuaſion charm'd,
Unnerv'd the ſtrong, the ſteel'd diſarm'd;

No ſafety ev'n the flying find,
Who, vent'rous, look but once behind.
  Thus was the much-admiring Maid,
While diſtant, more than half betray'd.
With ſmiles, and adulation bland,
They join'd her ſide, and ſeiz'd her hand;
Their touch envenom'd ſweets inſtill'd,
Her frame with new pulſations thrill'd;
While half conſenting, half denying,
Reluctant now, and now complying,
Amidſt a war of hopes, and fears,
Of trembling wiſhes, ſmiling tears,
Still down, and down, the winning Pair
Compell'd the ſtruggling, yielding Fair.
As when ſome ſtately veſſel, bound
To bleſt Arabia's diſtant ground,

Borne from her courses, haply lights
Where Barca's flow'ry clime invites,
Conceal'd around whose treach'rous land,
Lurk the dire rock, and dang'rous sand;
The pilot warns with sail and oar,
To shun the much suspected shore,
In vain; the tide, too subtly strong,
Still bears the wrestling bark along,
'Till found'ring, she resigns to fate,
And sinks, o'erwhelm'd, with all her freight.
So, baffling ev'ry bar to sin,
And heaven's own pilot, plac'd within,
Along the devious, smooth descent,
With pow'rs increasing as they went,
The Dames accustom'd to subdue,
As with a rapid current drew,

And

And o'er the fatal bounds convey'd
The loſt, the long reluctant Maid.

Here ſtop, ye fair ones, and beware,
Nor ſend your fond affections there;
Yet, yet your darling, now deplor'd,
May turn, to you, and heav'n, reſtor'd;
Till then, with weeping honour wait,
The ſervant of her better fate,
With honour, left upon the ſhore,
Her friend, and handmaid, now no more;
Nor, with the guilty world, upbraid
The fortunes of a wretch betray'd;
But o'er her failing caſt a veil,
Remembring, you yourſelves are frail.

And now, from all-enquiring light,
Faſt fled the conſcious ſhades of night;

The

The Damſel, from a ſhort repoſe,
Confounded at her plight, aroſe.
  As when, with ſlumb'rous weight oppreſs'd,
Some wealthy miſer ſinks to reſt,
Where felons eye the glitt'ring prey,
And ſteal his hoard of joys away;
He, borne where golden Indus ſtreams,
Of pearl, and quarry'd di'mond dreams,
Like Midas, turns the glebe to oar,
And ſtands all wrapt amidſt his ſtore,
But wakens, naked, and deſpoil'd
Of that, for which his years had toil'd.
  So far'd the Nymph, her treaſure flown,
And turn'd, like Niobe, to ſtone,
Within, without, obſcure, and void,
She felt all ravag'd, all deſtroy'd.

And, O thou curs'd, insidious coast!
Are these the blessings thou can'st boast?
These, virtue! these the joys they find,
Who leave thy heav'n-topt hills behind?
Shade me, ye pines, ye caverns, hide,
Ye mountains, cover me, she cry'd!

Her trumpet slander rais'd on high,
And told the tydings to the sky;
Contempt discharged a living dart,
A side-long viper to her heart;
Reproach breath'd poisons o'er her face,
And soil'd, and blasted ev'ry grace;
Officious shame, her handmaid new,
Still turn'd the mirror to her view,
While those, in crimes the deepest dy'd,
Approach'd to whiten at her side,

And ev'ry lewd, insulting dame
Upon her folly rose to fame.

What should she do? Attempt once more
To gain the late-deserted shore?
So trusting, back the Mourner flew,
As fast the train of fiends pursue.

Again the farther shore's attain'd,
Again the land of virtue gain'd;
But echo gathers in the wind,
And shows her instant foes behind.
Amaz'd, with headlong speed she tends,
Where late she left an host of friends;
Alas! those shrinking friends decline,
Nor longer own that form divine,
With fear they mark the following cry,
And from the lonely Trembler fly,

Or backward drive her on the coaſt,
Where peace was wreck'd, and honour loſt.
From earth, thus hoping aid in vain,
To heav'n, not daring to complain,
No truce by hoſtile clamour giv'n,
And from the face of friendſhip driv'n,
The Nymph ſunk proſtrate on the ground,
With all her weight of woes around.

Enthron'd within a circling ſky,
Upon a mount, o'er mountains high,
All radiant ſate, as in a ſhrine,
Virtue, firſt effluence divine;
Far, far above the ſcenes of woe,
That ſhut this cloud-wrapt world below;
Superior goddeſs, eſſence bright,
Beauty of uncreated light,

Whom

Whom ſhould mortality ſurvey,
As doom'd upon a certain day,
The breath of frailty muſt expire,
The world diſſolve in living fire,
The gems of heav'n, and ſolar flame
Be quench'd by her eternal beam,
And nature, quick'ning in her eye,
To riſe a new-born phœnix, die.

Hence, unreveal'd to mortal view,
A veil around her form ſhe threw,
Which three ſad ſiſters of the ſhade
Pain, Care, and Melancholy made.

Thro' this her all-enquiring eye,
Attentive from her ſtation high,
Beheld, abandon'd to deſpair,
The ruins of her fav'rite fair;

And

And with a voice, whoſe awful ſound
Appal'd the guilty world around,
Bid the tumultuous winds be ſtill,
To number's bow'd each liſt'ning hill,
Uncurl'd the ſurging of the main,
And ſmooth'd the thorny bed of pain,
The golden harp of heav'n ſhe ſtrung,
And thus the tuneful goddeſs ſung.

Lovely Penitent, ariſe,
Come, and claim thy kindred ſkies,
Come, thy ſiſter angels ſay
Thou haſt wept thy ſtains away.

Let experience now decide
'Twixt the good, and evil try'd,
In the ſmooth, enchanted ground,
Say, unfold the treaſures found.

Structures

Structures, rais'd by morning dreams,
Sands, that trip the flitting ſtreams,
Down, that anchors on the air,
Clouds, that paint their changes there.

Seas, that ſmoothly dimpling lie,
While the ſtorm impends on high,
Showing, in an obvious glaſs,
Joys that in poſſeſſion paſs;

Tranſient, fickle, light, and gay,
Flatt'ring, only to betray;
What, alas, can life contain!
Life! like all it's circles——vain.

Will the ſtork, intending reſt,
On the billow build her neſt?
Will the bee demand his ſtore
From the bleak, and bladeleſs ſhore?

Man

Man alone, intent to ſtray,
Ever turns from wiſdom's way,
Lays up wealth in foreign land,
Sows the ſea, and plows the ſand.

Soon this elemental maſs,
Soon th' incumb'ring world ſhall paſs,
Form be wrapt in waſting fire,
Time be ſpent, and life expire.

Then, ye boaſted works of men,
Where is your aſylum then?
Sons of pleaſure, ſons of care,
Tell me mortals, tell me where?

Gone, like traces on the deep,
Like a ſcepter, graſp'd in ſleep,
Dews, exhal'd from morning glades,
Melting ſnows, and gliding ſhades.

Paſs the world, and what's behind?
Virtue's gold, by fire refin'd;
From an univerſe deprav'd,
From the wreck of nature ſav'd.]

Like the life-ſupporting grain,
Fruit of patience, and of pain,
On the ſwain's autumnal day,
Winnow'd from the chaff away.

Little trembler, fear no more,
Thou haſt plenteous crops in ſtore,
Seed, by genial ſorrows ſown,
More than all thy ſcorners own.

What tho' hoſtile earth deſpiſe,
Heav'n beholds with gentler eyes;
Heav'n thy friendleſs ſteps ſhall guide,
Chear thy hours, and guard thy ſide.

When

When the fatal trump ſhall ſound,
When th' immortals pour around,
Heav'n ſhall thy return atteſt,
Hail'd by myriads of the bleſs'd.

Little native of the ſkies,
Lovely penitent, ariſe;
Calm thy boſom, clear thy brow,
Virtue is thy ſiſter now.

More delightful are my woes,
Than the rapture, pleaſure knows:
Richer far the weeds I bring,
Than the robes, that grace a king.

On my wars, of ſhorteſt date,
Crowns of endleſs triumph wait;
On my cares a period bleſs'd;
On my toils, eternal reſt.

Come, with virtue at thy ſide,
Come, be ev'ry bar defy'd,
'Till we gain our native ſhore,
Siſter, come, and turn no more.

148

Fab. 16.

F. Hayman inv. et delin. J. S. Ravenet Sculp.

FABLE XVI.

Love *and* Vanity.

THE breezy morning breath'd perfume,
The wak'ning flow'rs unveil'd their bloom,
Up with the sun, from short repose,
Gay health, and lusty labour rose,
The milkmaid carol'd at her pail,
And shepherds whistled o'er the dale;
When Love, who led a rural life,
Remote from bustle, state, and strife,

Forth from his thatch'd-roof'd cottage ſtray'd,
And ſtroll'd along the dewy glade.

A Nymph, who lightly trip'd it by,
To quick attention turn'd his eye,
He mark'd the geſture of the Fair,
Her ſelf-ſufficient grace and air,
Her ſteps, that mincing meant to pleaſe,
Her ſtudy'd negligence, and eaſe;
And curious to enquire what meant
This thing of prettineſs, and paint,
Approaching ſpoke, and bow'd obſervant;
The Lady, ſlightly,—Sir, your ſervant.

Such beauty in ſo rude a place!
Fair one, you do the country grace;
At court, no doubt, the public care,
But Love has ſmall acquaintance there.

Yes,

Yes, Sir, reply'd the flutt'ring Dame,
This form confesses whence it came;
But dear variety, you know,
Can make us pride, and pomp forego.
My Name is Vanity. I sway
The utmost islands of the sea;
Within my court all honour centers;
I raise the meanest soul that enters,
Endow with latent gifts, and graces,
And model fools, for posts and places.

As Vanity appoints at pleasure,
The world receives it's weight, and measure;
Hence all the grand concerns of life,
Joys, cares, plagues, passions, peace and strife.

Reflect how far my pow'r prevails,
When I step in, where nature fails,

And ev'ry breach of ſenſe repairing,
Am bounteous ſtill, where heav'n is ſparing.
But chief in all their arts, and airs,
Their playing, painting, pouts, and pray'rs,
Their various habits, and complexions,
Fits, frolicks, foibles, and perfections,
Their robing, curling and adorning,
From noon to night, from night to morning,
From ſix to ſixty, ſick or ſound,
I rule the female world around.
Hold there a moment, Cupid cry'd,
Nor boaſt dominion quite ſo wide.
Was there no province to invade,
But that by Love, and meekneſs ſway'd?
All other empire I reſign,
But be the ſphere of beauty mine.

For

For in the downy lawn of reſt,
That opens on a woman's breaſt,
Attended by my peaceful train,
I chuſe to live, and chuſe to reign.

Far-ſighted faith I bring along,
And truth, above an army ſtrong,
And chaſtity, of icy mold,
Within the burning tropics cold,
And lowlineſs, to whoſe mild brow,
The pow'r and pride of nations bow,
And modeſty, with downcaſt eye,
That lends the morn her virgin dye,
And innocence, array'd in light,
And honour, as a tow'r upright?
With ſweetly winning graces, more
Than poets ever dreamt of yore,

In

In unaffected conduct free,
All ſmiling ſiſters, three times three,
And roſy peace, the cherub bleſs'd,
That nightly ſings us all to reſt.

Hence, from the bud of nature's prime,
From the firſt ſtep of infant time,
Woman, the world's appointed light,
Has ſkirted ev'ry ſhade with white;
Has ſtood for imitation high,
To ev'ry heart and ev'ry eye;
From antient deeds of fair renown,
Has brought her bright memorials down;
To time affix'd perpetual youth,
And form'd each tale of love and truth.

Upon a new Promethean plan,
She moulds the eſſence of a man,

Tempers his maſs, his genius fires,
And as a better ſoul, inſpires.

The rude ſhe ſoftens, warms the cold,
Exalts the meek, and checks the bold,
Calls ſloth from his ſupine repoſe,
Within the coward's boſom glows,
Of pride unplumes the lofty creſt,
Bids baſhful merit ſtand confeſs'd,
And like coarſe metal from the mines,
Collects, irradiates, and refines.

The gentle ſcience, ſhe imparts,
All manners ſmooths, informs all hearts;
From her ſweet influence are felt,
Paſſions that pleaſe, and thoughts that melt;
To ſtormy rage ſhe bids controul,
And ſinks ſerenely on the ſoul,

Softens Deucalion's flinty race,
And tunes the warring world to peace.

Thus arm'd to all that's light, and vain,
And freed from thy fantaſtic chain,
She fills the ſphere, by heav'n aſſign'd,
And rul'd by me, o'er-rules mankind.

He ſpoke. The nymph impatient ſtood,
And laughing, thus her ſpeech renew'd.

And pray, Sir, may I be ſo bold
To hope your pretty tale is told;
And next demand, without a cavil,
What new Utopia do you travel?——
Upon my Word, theſe high-flown fancies
Shew depth of learning—in romances.

Why, what unfaſhion'd ſtuff you tell us,
Of buckram dames, and tiptoe fellows!

Go, child; and when you're grown maturer,
You'll ſhoot your next opinion ſurer.

O ſuch a pretty knack at painting!
And all for ſoftning, and for ſainting!
Gueſs now, who can, a ſingle feature,
Thro' the whole piece of female nature!
Then mark! my looſer hand may fit
The lines, too coarſe for Love to hit.

'Tis ſaid that woman, prone to changing,
Thro' all the rounds of folly ranging,
On life's uncertain ocean riding,
No reaſon, rule, nor rudder guiding,
Is like the comet's wand'ring light,
Eccentric, ominous, and bright,
Trackleſs, and ſhifting as the wind,
A ſea, whoſe fathom none can find,

A moon,

A moon, ſtill changing, and revolving,
A riddle, paſt all human ſolving.
A bliſs, a plague, a heav'n, a hell,
A——ſomething, that no man can tell.
Now learn a ſecret from a friend,
But keep your council, and attend.
Tho' in their tempers thought ſo diſtant,
Nor with their ſex, nor ſelves conſiſtent,
'Tis but the diff'rence of a name,
And ev'ry woman is the ſame.
For as the world however vary'd,
And through unnumber'd changes carry'd,
Of elemental modes, and forms,
Clouds, meteors, colours, calms and ſtorms,
Tho' in a thouſand ſuits array'd,
Is of one ſubject matter made;

So, Sir, a woman's conſtitution,
The world's enigma, finds ſolution,
And let her form be what you will,
I am the ſubject eſſence ſtill.

With the firſt ſpark of female ſenſe,
The ſpeck of being, I commence,
Within the womb make freſh advances,
And dictate future qualms, and fancies;
Thence in the growing form expand,
With childhood travel hand in hand,
And give a taſte of all their joys,
In gewgaws, rattles, pomp, and noiſe.

And now, familiar, and unaw'd,
I ſend the flutt'ring ſoul abroad.
Prais'd for her ſhape, her air, her mein,
The little goddeſs, and the queen,

'Takes at her infant ſhrine oblation,
And drinks ſweet draughts of addulation.
Now blooming, tall, erect, and fair,
To dreſs, becomes her darling care;
The realms of beauty then I bound,
I ſwell the hoop's enchanted round,
Shrink in the waiſt's deſcending ſize,
Heav'd in the ſnowy boſom, riſe,
High on the floating lappet ſail
Or curl'd in treſſes, kiſs the gale.
Then to her glaſs I lead the fair,
And ſhew the lovely idol there,
Where, ſtruck as by divine emotion,
She bows with moſt ſincere devotion,
And numbering every beauty o'er
In ſecret bids the world adore.

Then

Then all for parking, and parading,
Coquetting, dancing, masquerading;
For balls, plays, courts, and crouds what passion!
And churches, sometimes—if the fashion;
For woman's sense of right, and wrong
Is rul'd by the almighty throng;
Still turns to each meander tame,
And swims, the straw of ev'ry stream.
Her soul intrinsic worth rejects,
Accomplish'd only in defects;
Such excellence is her ambition,
Folly, her wisest acquisition,
And ev'n from pity, and disdain,
She'll cull some reason to be vain.

Thus, Sir, from ev'ry form, and feature,
The wealth, and wants of female nature,

And ev'n from vice, which you'd admire,
I gather fewel to my fire;
And on the very base of shame
Erect my monument of fame.

Let me another truth attempt,
Of which your godship has not dreamt.

Those shining virtues, which you muster,
Whence think you they derive their lustre?
From native honour, and devotion?
O yes, a mighty likely notion?
Trust me, from titled dames to spinners,
'Tis I make saints, whoe'er makes sinners;
'Tis I instruct them to withdraw,
And hold presumptuous man in awe;
For female worth, as I inspire,
In just degrees, still mounts the higher,

And

And virtue, ſo extremely nice,
Demands long toil, and mighty price;
Like Sampſon's pillars, fix'd elate,
I bear the ſex's tott'ring ſtate,
Sap theſe, and in a moment's ſpace,
Down ſinks the fabric to its baſe.

Alike from titles, and from toys,
I ſpring, the fount of female joys;
In ev'ry widow, wife, and miſs,
The ſole artificer of bliſs;
From them each tropic I explore,
I cleave the ſand of ev'ry ſhore;
To them uniting Indias ſail,
Sabæa breathes her fartheſt gale:
For them the bullion I refine,
Dig ſenſe, and virtue from the mine,

And from the bowels of invention,
Spin out the various arts you mention.
Nor bliſs alone my pow'rs beſtow,
They hold the ſovereign balm of woe;
Beyond the Stoic's boaſted art,
I ſooth the heavings of the heart;
To pain give ſplendor, and relief,
And gild the pallid face of grief.
Alike the palace, and the plain
Admit the glories of my reign;
Thro' ev'ry age, in ev'ry nation,
Taſte, talents, tempers, ſtate, and ſtation,
Whate'er a woman ſays, I ſay;
Whate'er a woman ſpends, I pay;
Alike I fill, and empty bags,
Flutter in finery, and rags,

With light coquets thro' folly range,
And with the prude difdain to change.
And now you'd think, 'twixt you, and I,
That things were ripe for a reply——
But foft, and while I'm in the mood,
Kindly permit me to conclude,
Their utmoft mazes to unravel,
And touch the fartheft ftep they travel.
When ev'ry pleafure's run aground,
And folly tir'd thro' many a round,
The nymph, conceiving difcontent hence,
May ripen to an hour's repentance,
And vapours, fhed in pious moifture,
Difmifs her to a church, or cloyfter;
Then on I lead her, with devotion
Confpicuous in her drefs, and motion,

Inſpire the heav'nly-breathing air,
Roll up the lucid eye in pray'r,
Soften the voice, and in the face
Look melting harmony, and grace.
  Thus far extends my friendly pow'r,
Nor quits her in her lateſt hour;
The couch of decent pain I ſpread,
In form recline her languid head,
Her thoughts I methodize in death,
And part not, with her parting breath;
Then do I ſet, in order bright,
A length of funeral pomp to ſight,
The glitt'ring tapers, and attire,
The plumes, that whiten o'er her bier;
And laſt, preſenting to her eye
Angelic fineries on high,

To ſcenes of painted bliſs I waft her,
And form the heav'n ſhe hopes hereafter.

In truth, rejoin'd love's gentle god,
You've gone a tedious length of road,
And ſtrange, in all the toilſome way,
No houſe of kind refreſhment lay,
No nymph, whoſe virtues might have tempted,
To hold her from her ſex exempted.

For one, we'll never quarrel, man;
Take her, and keep her, if you can;
And pleas'd I yield to your petition,
Since ev'ry fair, by ſuch permiſſion,
Will hold herſelf the one ſelected,
And ſo my ſyſtem ſtands protected.

O deaf to virtue, deaf to glory,
To truths divinely vouch'd in ſtory!

The godhead in his zeal return'd,
And kindling at her malice burn'd.
Then ſweetly rais'd his voice, and told
Of heav'nly nymphs, rever'd of old;
Hypſipyle, who ſav'd her ſire,
And Portia's love, approv'd by fire,
Alike Penelope was quoted,
Nor laurel'd Daphne paſs'd unnoted,
Nor Laodamia's fatal garter,
Nor fam'd Lucretia, honour's martyr,
Alceſte's voluntary ſteel,
And Catherine, ſmiling on the wheel.
But who can hope to plant conviction
Where cavil grows on contradiction?
Some ſhe evades, or diſavows,
Demurs to all, and none allows;

A kind

A kind of antient thing call'd fables!
And thus the goddeſs turn'd the tables.

Now both in argument grew high,
And choler flaſh'd from either eye;
Nor wonder each refus'd to yield
The conqueſt of ſo fair a field.

When happily arrived in view
A Goddeſs, whom our grandames knew,
Of aſpect grave, and ſober gaite,
Majeſtic, aweful, and ſedate,
As heav'ns autumnal eve ſerene,
When not a cloud o'ercaſts the ſcene;
Once Prudence call'd, a matron fam'd,
And in old Rome, Cornelia nam'd.
Quick at a venture, both agree
To leave their ſtrife to her decree.

And

And now by each the facts were ſtated,
In form and manner as related,
The caſe was ſhort. They crav'd opinion,
Which held o'er females chief dominion:
When thus the Goddeſs, anſwering mild,
Firſt ſhook her gracious head, and ſmil'd.

Alas, how willing to comply,
Yet how unfit a judge am I!
In times of golden date, 'tis true,
I ſhar'd the fickle ſex with you;
But from their preſence long precluded,
Or held as one, whoſe form intruded,
Full fifty annual ſuns can tell,
Prudence has bid the ſex farewel.

In this dilemma what to do,
Or who to think of, neither knew;

For

For both, ſtill biaſs'd in opinion,
And arrogant of ſole dominion,
Were forc'd to hold the caſe compounded,
Or leave the quarrel where they found it.
  When in the nick, a rural fair,
Of inexperienc'd gaite, and air,
Who ne'er had croſs'd the neighb'ring lake,
Nor ſeen the world, beyond a wake,
With cambric coif, and kerchief clean,
Tript lightly by them o'er the green.
  Now, now! cry'd love's triumphant Child,
And at approaching conqueſt ſmil'd,
If Vanity will once be guided,
Our diff'rence ſoon may be decided;
Behold yon wench, a fit occaſion
To try your force of gay perſuation.

Go

Go you, while I retire aloof,
Go, put thofe boafted pow'rs to proof;
And if your prevalence of art
Tranfcends my yet unerring dart,
I give the fav'rite conteft o'er,
And ne'er will boaft my empire more.

At once, fo faid, and fo confented;
And well our goddefs feem'd contented,
Nor paufing, made a moment's ftand,
But tript, and took the girl in hand.

Meanwhile the Godhead, unalarm'd,
As one to each occafion arm'd,
Forth from his quiver cull'd a dart,
That erft had wounded many a heart;
Then bending, drew it to the head;
The bow-ftring twang'd, the arrow fled,

And

And, to her ſecret ſoul addreſs'd,
Transfix'd the whiteneſs of her breaſt.

But here the Dame, whoſe guardian care
Had to a moment watch'd the fair,
At once her pocket mirror drew,
And held the wonder full in view;
As quickly rang'd in order bright,
A thouſand beauties ruſh to ſight,
A world of charms till now unknown,
A world reveal'd to her alone;
Enraptur'd ſtands the love-ſick maid,
Suſpended o'er the darling ſhade,
Here only fixes to admire,
And centers ev'ry fond deſire.

FINIS.

www.ingramcontent.com/pod-product-compliance
Lightning Source LLC
Chambersburg PA
CBHW020606030726
47497CB00007B/2111
9783744768092